# AUSTRALIAN FROGS AND REPTILES

NATURE kids

Mason Crest Publishers
www.masoncrest.com
Philadelphia

**Mason Crest Publishers
370 Reed Road
Broomall, PA 19008
(866) MCP-BOOK (toll free)**

First printing

ISBN 1-59084-216-2

Library of Congress Cataloging-in-Publication Data on file at the Library of Congress

First published by Steve Parish Publishing Pty Ltd
PO Box 1058, Archerfield BC
Queensland 4108, Australia
© Copyright Steve Parish Publishing Pty Ltd

Photography: Steve Parish

Photographic Assistance: Darran Leal

Front Cover: Frilled Lizard (photo Stan Breeden)

Title Page: Red-Eyed Tree Frog (photo Steve Parish)
    p. 16, 22-23: Hans & Judy Beste
    pp. 4-5, 8, 8-9, 19, 28: Darran Leal
    pp. 14, 43, 44 (top), 45, 46-47: Ian Morris
    pp. 10, 42: Stan Breeden

Printed in Jordan

Writing, editing, design, and production by Steve Parish Publishing Pty Ltd, Australia

# CONTENTS

Use of Capital Letters for Animal Names in this book
An animal's official common name begins with a capital letter.
Otherwise the name begins with a lowercase letter.

# WHAT ARE FROGS?

Frogs are animals with soft, moist skins. Many have large hind legs. When they hurry, they leap rather than run.

Most female frogs lay their eggs in a damp place or in water. The tadpoles that hatch from the eggs breathe through gills and have tails. Gradually, they lose their tails and gills, grow legs, and become adult frogs.

A male and a larger female Fletcher's Frog mating. ▶

▲ The larger Striped Marsh Frog tadpole is almost a frog.

4

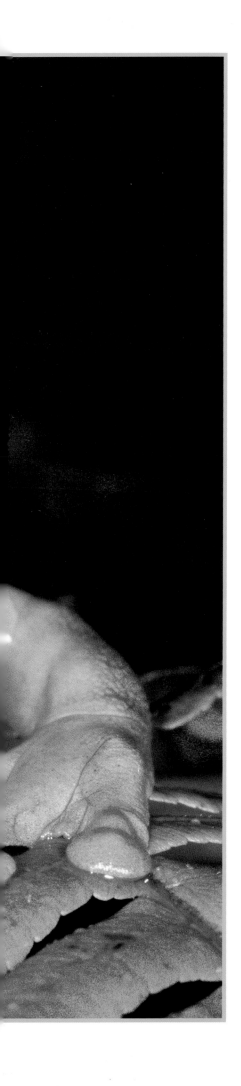

# FROGS THAT CLIMB

Frogs that live in trees and in cracks in rocks have to be good climbers. Many have fingers and toes that end in round, flat pads. These help them cling to smooth surfaces. Some can even climb up glass.

The best time to see all sorts of frogs is during the first heavy rain after a dry spell. At this time, male frogs find pools of water. They sit nearby and call loudly for mates.

◀ A Red-Eyed Tree Frog

▲ A Bleating Tree Frog calling for a mate.

# FROGS THAT BURROW

In hot weather, some frogs burrow into the ground. When rain falls, they leave their burrows. Then, they look for food and mates.

All frogs have tiny pockets in their skins called glands. These make liquid to keep the skin damp. Some frogs can ooze nasty-tasting or poisonous liquid from these glands. If an enemy bites this sort of frog, it will quickly spit it out again.

This Moaning Frog protects itself by oozing white liquid. ▶

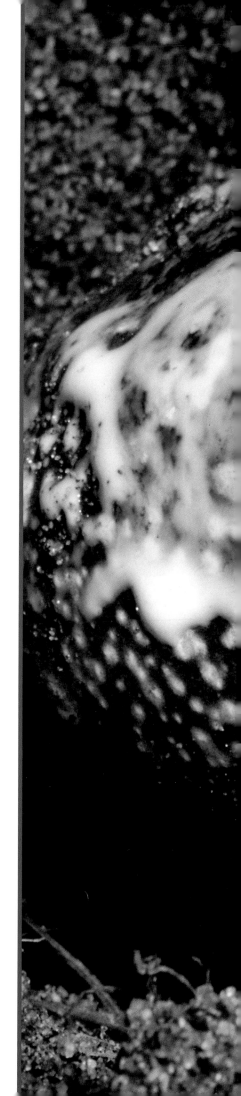

▲ The frog burrows into the ground backwards.

# GOOD PARENTS

▲ The Striped Burrowing Frog breeds in spring.

Some frogs look after their eggs. Sometimes, they even care for their tadpoles.

The Corroboree Frog lives in mossy swamps in the Australian Alps. A female lays her eggs in damp moss. Then, a parent stays with the eggs until the tadpoles turn to frogs.

Some female frogs paddle the water while mating. They whip up bubble rafts that protect their eggs. In the picture on pages 4 and 5, the female has made a bubble raft.

◄ This Corroboree Frog's eggs have tadpoles inside them.

# VANISHING FROGS

▲ The female Northern Gastric-Brooding Frog's tadpoles develop inside her stomach. When they are big enough, they climb out of her mouth. This frog has not been seen since 1985.

Many of Australia's frogs are becoming rare. Some have not been seen for many years.

Many things can hurt frogs. They need good rain to breed. In a drought, many frogs will die. They can be harmed by the sun's rays that give humans sunburn.

When swamps are drained, frogs disappear. Their tadpoles are harmed by weed killers and other chemicals.

The introduced Cane Toad eats frogs. It has poison glands in its skin. It is also causing Australia's frogs to disappear.

◄ The Cane Toad is a danger to Australian frogs.

# FROGS AND THEIR ENEMIES

▲ A Keelback Snake swallowing a Green Tree Frog. This snake is not venomous, and the frog may still escape.

The skin colors of this Tyler's Frog help it hide ▶ from enemies. The yellow on its sides will show as a flash of color when the frog jumps away.

Snakes, birds, freshwater turtles, and Cane Toads all eat frogs. Big frogs eat smaller frogs. However, frogs have many ways of escaping these enemies.

A frog's skin colors help hide it. When it jumps away from danger, it may flash bright patches. These can scare off the frog's enemy while it escapes.

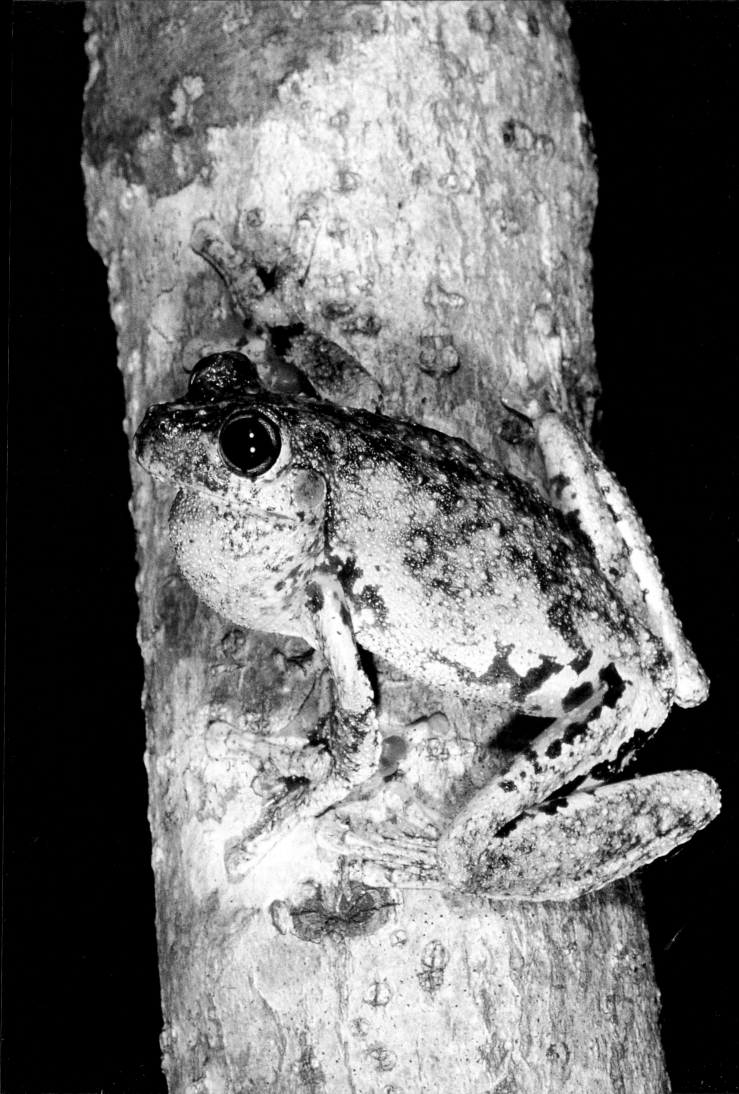

# WHAT ARE REPTILES?

Turtles, crocodiles, lizards, and snakes are all reptiles. They have dry skins that are covered with scales. Sometimes, the scales are soft, but often they are hard.

Most reptiles cannot heat up their bodies from inside in the way that birds and mammals do.

Instead, they get warm in the rays of the sun. When they become too hot, they shelter from the sun.

A few reptiles eat plants. However, most eat other animals. The animals that are caught are called "prey."

The Carpet Python has pits in its lips that sense heat from the bodies of prey. ▷

▲ A Boyd's Forest Dragon with its eggs. Some reptiles lay eggs; others give birth to babies.

▲ The Saltwater Crocodile has a broad snout. Its teeth are thick and strong.

▲ The Freshwater Crocodile has a slender snout. Its teeth are thin and needle-like.

# CROCODILES

Crocodiles are big reptiles that live mostly in water. When they swim, they move their strong tails from side to side. A crocodile's back is protected by bony scales.

Crocodiles come on to land to warm themselves in sunlight and to lay their eggs. A female crocodile stays near her nest until the young ones hatch. Then she takes them to the water.

The Freshwater Crocodile eats fish and does not harm humans. It is found in rivers and billabongs in Northern Australia.

Saltwater, or Estuarine, Crocodiles can grow to around 19 feet long. They are found around the coast and in rivers in Northern Australia. They are fierce and strong meat-eaters and can be dangerous to humans.

▲ A Saltwater Crocodile warming its body in the sunlight. This action is called basking.

# MARINE TURTLES

The body of a turtle is protected by a hard shell. Its head, tail, and legs poke out between the top and bottom of the shell.

Marine turtles spend nearly all their lives in the ocean. Their limbs are flippers.

The females drag themselves onto beaches to dig pits into which to lay their eggs. The hatchling turtles must scurry down to the sea and swim away. It will be many years before they are old enough to breed.

These tiny Flatback Turtles have only just hatched. ▶

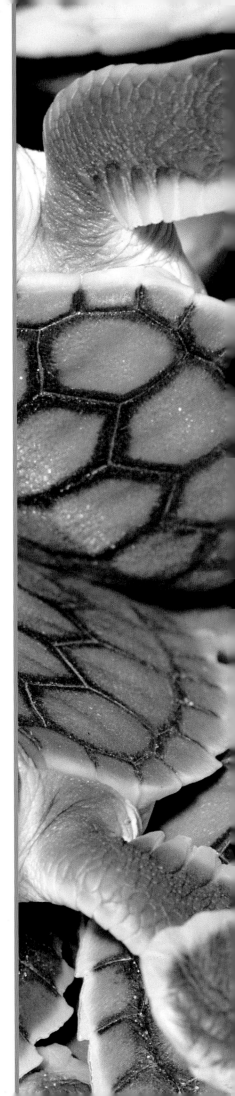

▲ A diver swimming near a Green Turtle.

# FRESHWATER TURTLES

A few of Australia's freshwater turtles have flippers. Most have strong legs, and their webbed feet have claws.

Sometimes, the creeks and waterholes that turtles live in dry up. Some turtles will try to walk overland to deeper pools.

Other turtles will sleep in holes they have dug in the mud. When rain comes, they wake up again and come out of hiding.

Most freshwater turtles eat fish, crayfish, frogs, insects, and even small waterbirds. A few eat fruit that has fallen into the water.

▲ A group of Brisbane Short-Necked Turtles on a log, basking in the sunlight.

▲ Most freshwater turtles have clawed, webbed feet. This is an Eastern Snake-Necked Turtle.

# GECKOS

Geckos are soft-skinned lizards. Their fingers and toes end in pads or claws. Each big eye is covered by a see-through goggle. This is the gecko's fixed lower eyelid. A gecko must lick its eyes to keep them clean.

A gecko's tail has a narrow part near the body. When an enemy attacks, the gecko drops its tail and runs away. The tail grows back again.

Geckos hunt insects and other small creatures. Some geckos eat other lizards.

◀ A Marbled Velvet Gecko hunting at night.

▲ The Leaf-Tailed Gecko blends with the bark behind it.

This gecko, a Three-lined Knob-tail, is hunting at night. During the day, it hides in a burrow it has dug in the sand. This stops its soft body drying out. When this type of gecko has had good hunting, it stores fat in its tail. When it cannot find much food, its body uses this fat for energy.

# LEGLESS LIZARDS

Legless lizards look like snakes, but have no fangs and cannot hurt humans. When they are frightened, some may rear up, hiss, and pretend to strike. If they are touched, they may squeak or shed the ends of their tails.

Most legless lizards eat insects, spiders, and sometimes flower nectar. However, Burton's Legless Lizard eats other lizards. It has a sloping head, a long snout, satiny scales, and scaly flaps in place of hind legs.

The Western Scaly-Foot looks and behaves like a little snake. ▶
Unlike a snake, however, it has earholes.

▲ Burton's Legless Lizard has many different color forms.

# DRAGON LIZARDS

Dragon lizards have rough scales. Many dragon lizards have crests of skin on their backs. Some have loose skin around their necks. They puff this skin out when signalling other dragons or trying to bluff their enemies.

Dragons can change the color of their skins. They turn darker when they bask in the sun. When two males fight, they flash bright patches of skin.

Dragons can move fast. Some of them even get up on their hind legs to run.

◀ The Southern Forest Dragon is a rainforest lizard.

▲ The Eastern Water Dragon lives near creeks.

# DRAGONS IN THE DESERT

Many dragon lizards live in deserts. During the hottest part of the day, some hide in burrows. Others shelter under bushes or between rocks. When it is cooler, they roam the desert, hunting for insects, spiders, and other prey.

▲ The Central Netted Ground Dragon is a fast runner. Its home is a burrow it has dug in the sand.

Desert dragons have a strange way of getting water. During the cool night, dew collects on their rough scales. When the drops are big enough, they trickle down between the scales and end up in the dragon's mouth.

▲ This Bearded Dragon is basking in the sun.

▲ The Thorny Devil eats small black ants. The spikes on its skin are softer than they seem.

# MONITORS

Monitors are large lizards whose rough skins are covered with tiny scales. Strong legs and sharp claws help them run fast and climb well. They may lash their whip-like tails to defend themselves. Monitor lizards are also known as goannas.

Monitors flick out their forked tongues to taste the air. They can track prey animals by the scent the animals leave behind.

The Lace Monitor can become used to humans. Sometimes, it will visit campsites looking for food.

▲ Merten's Water Monitor catches its food in creeks and rivers.

Lace Monitor ▶

The Sand Monitor is found over most of mainland Australia. Here it is resting among spiny spinifex plants.

# SKINKS

There are many different sorts of skinks. Some, like the Shingleback, are quite big. Others, like the spotted lizards, are quite small. They usually have smooth, shiny scales. Some have small legs, and a few have only hind legs. Some skinks have almost no legs at all. They have slick scales and wriggle through the sand or under leaves.

Small skinks may shed their tails when attacked. The wriggling tail is eaten by the attacker, and the skink runs to safety.

A Shingleback bluffing an enemy. ▷

▲ Small, shiny-scaled lizards are usually skinks.

# PYTHONS

Snakes are long, slender reptiles that have no legs.

Pythons are snakes with strong, muscular bodies. They have many sharp teeth.

When a python finds a prey animal, it bites it hard. Then it coils around it and squeezes it to death. Like all snakes, a python swallows its prey whole.

After a python has eaten, it coils up and sleeps. After a big meal, it will not need to eat again for a long time.

◄ The Green Python lives in northern rainforests.

A Diamond Python ▲

# REAR FANGED SNAKES

Many Australian snakes have sharp, hollow teeth called fangs. Through these fangs, they inject venom into their prey. This venom kills the prey so the snake can swallow it.

Some snakes, such as the Brown Tree Snake, have short fangs at the backs of their mouths. Their venom is weak. They are not a danger to humans.

Some Australian snakes have solid teeth and no venom at all.

The Green Tree Snake is one of these harmless snakes. It may be colored green, blue, or bronze, with a green or yellow belly. It lives in gardens and bush and eats frogs and lizards.

▲ The Northern Brown Tree Snake eats birds that it catches when they are sleeping at night.

The Green Tree Snake has solid teeth and no venom. It eats frogs and lizards. ▶

▲ This Western Brown Snake is hunting. Like all snakes, it detects scents with its forked tongue.

▲ The Eastern Tiger Snake lives near water. It is one of Australia's most dangerous snakes.

44

# FRONT FANGED SNAKES

▲ A Northern Death Adder injecting venom into a gecko.

Australia's most dangerous snakes have hollow fangs at the front corners of their upper jaws. These work like doctors' needles.

When the snake bites, venom from a gland in its jaw is forced into the wound.

These snakes have powerful venom. The prey soon dies and can be then swallowed.

If a human is bitten, an injection of antivenom will work against the snake venom. This should save the person's life.

# FiLE SNAKES AND BLiND SNAKES

File snakes live in swamps and mangroves across Northern Australia. They have rough, loose skins; eat fish; and are not venomous.

Blind snakes are small, and their round bodies are covered with shiny scales. Their eyes are tiny. They can probably only tell the difference between day and night. These harmless snakes live in the soil or under leaves, logs, or stones. Some eat ants or termites. They live in ant or termite mounds.

An Aboriginal hunter with two Arafura File Snakes. ▶

▲ A Blackish Blind Snake looks like a shiny worm.

# SEASNAKES

A seasnake swims by rippling its body from side to side. Some seasnakes have flat tails, like paddles.

Seasnakes usually eat fish and fish eggs. Many of these snakes have rough scales. These scales help them hold a fish until the venom they have injected has taken effect.

Seasnakes breathe air, but most never leave the ocean. Their young ones are born underwater. If a snake is found on the beach, humans should leave it alone. Seasnake venom is quite powerful.

◀ A Golden Seasnake underwater.

▲ A seasnake on the beach. Its head is to the left.

# INDEX OF ANIMALS PICTURED

# FURTHER READING & INTERNET RESOURCES

For more information on Australia's animals, check out the following books and Web sites.

Reilly, Pauline and Will Roland (illustrator). Frillneck: An Australian Dragon. (August 1993) Jarrold Publishers; ISBN: 0864174144

This book explains the life cycle of a Frilled Lizard, complete with beautiful illustrations.

Roth, Susan L. The Biggest Frog in Australia. (April 2000) Aladdin Paperbacks; ISBN: 0689833148

This is a retelling of a classic Australian folktale. When the biggest frog in Australia wakes up thirsty and drinks all the water, it's up to the other animals to make him laugh and bring water back to Australia.

Langeland, Deidre, Frank Ordaz (illustrator), and Ranye Kaye (narrator). *Kangaroo Island: The Story of an Australian Mallee Forest.* (April 1998) Soundprints Corp. Audio; ISBN: 156899544X

As morning comes to Kangaroo Island following a thunderstorm, a mother kangaroo finds her lost baby, and a burned eucalyptus tree sprouts buds and becomes a new home for animals. The cassette that comes with the book adds sounds of sea lions barking, sea gulls calling, crickets humming, and even a raging forest fire.

Paul, Tessa. *Down Under (Animal Trackers Around the World).* (May 1998) Crabtree Publishers; ISBN: 0865055963

The book features beautiful illustrations of each animal, its tracks, diet, and environment and includes interesting facts about how each animal lives. Australian animals featured include the platypus, the dingo, the kiwi, the kangaroo, the emu, the koala, the kookaburra, and the Tasmanian devil.

http://www.dlwc.nsw.gov.au/care/wetlands/facts/paa/frogs/litoria.html

This site contains a listing of frogs found in Australia's wetlands. The link for each frog provides an illustration as well as information on the species' general characteristics and habitat.

http://www.westernwildlife.com.au/frogs/index.htm

The Frog Files contains an extensive amount of information on the frogs of Western Australia. Links provide information on habitat, description, breeding—even the calls these animals make are described!

http://www.reptilepark.com.au/index.html

This Web site for The Australian Reptile Park contains information on all the animals in the park, including various reptiles and amphibians native to Australia. Basic information on many species is provided, such as habitat, description, and so on.

http://www.rainforest.org.au/

The Australian Rainforest Conservation Society is dedicated to protecting, repairing, and restoring the rainforests of Australia. Viewers to this site can learn about Australia's rainforests and what steps have been taken so far by the Society to accomplish their mission.

http://www.austrop.org.au/daintree.htm

Daintree Forest—a small area of coastal lowland rainforest—has most of the endangered rainforest creatures in Australia and is under immense pressure to be cleared for private home sites. Viewers to this site can read about the controversy surrounding this beautiful land and find out what they can do to help in this campaign

# NATURE KIDS SERIES

## Birdlife

Australia is home to some of the most interesting, colorful, and noisy birds on earth. Discover some of the many different types, including parrots, kingfishers, and owls.

## Frogs and Reptiles

Australia has a wide variety of environments, and there is at least one frog or reptile that calls each environment home. Discover the frogs and reptiles living in Australia.

## Kangaroos and Wallabies

The kangaroo is one of the most well-known Australian creatures. Learn interesting facts about kangaroos and wallabies, a close cousin.

## Marine Fish

The ocean surrounding Australia is home to all sorts of marine fish. Discover their interesting shapes, sizes, and colors, and learn about the different types of habitat in the ocean.

## Rainforest Animals

Australia's rainforests are home to a wide range of animals, including snakes, birds, frogs, and wallabies. Discover a few of the creatures that call the rainforests home.

## Rare & Endangered Wildlife

Animals all over the world need our help to keep from becoming extinct. Learn about the special creatures in Australia that are in danger of disappearing forever.

## Sealife

Australia is surrounded by sea. As a result, there is an amazing variety of life that lives in these waters. Dolphins, crabs, reef fish, and eels are just a few of the animals highlighted in this book.

## Wildlife

Australia is known for its unique creatures, such as the kangaroo and the koala. Read about these and other special creatures that call Australia home.